This book belongs to:

Rajaindeep
Singh

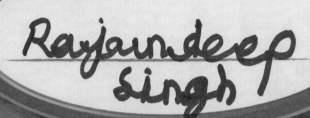

Imagination

Published by Scholastic Inc., 90 Old Sherman Turnpike, Danbury, CT 06816

SCHOLASTIC and associated logos are trademarks and/or registered trademarks of Scholastic Inc.

ISBN 0-7172-9873-6

Printed in the U.S.A.

First Scholastic Printing, June 2006

The Fastest Drawer in the West

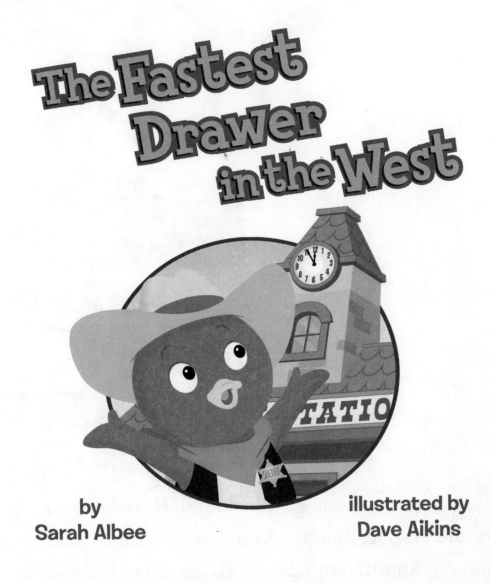

by
Sarah Albee

illustrated by
Dave Aikins

SCHOLASTIC INC.

New York Toronto London Auckland Sydney
Mexico City New Delhi Hong Kong Buenos Aires

It was a quiet morning in a sleepy Western town. Sheriff Pablo and Deputy Uniqua were doing a bit of cleaning. "Tarnation, Sheriff, am I proud to be your deputy!" said Deputy Uniqua admiringly, as she polished the trophy case. "Folks say you're the fastest drawer in the West."

"Aw, shucks, Deputy Uniqua,"
said the sheriff modestly, as he
dusted off another plaque.

FASTEST
DRAWER
IN THE WEST
★SHERIFF PABLO★

SHERIFF
PABLO
FASTEST DRAWER
IN THE WEST

Suddenly, Shopkeeper Tyrone hurried in. "Tasha the Kid is coming to town!" he yelled. "She's coming in on the noon train!"

"Did you say, *T-t-t-tasha the K-k-kid?*" stammered the sheriff.

"Yes, indeed," said Shopkeeper Tyrone. "She's a legend." He looked over his shoulder, and then whispered, "I know you're the fastest drawer *this* side of the Rio Grande, Sheriff, but I hear folks say *she's* the fastest drawer on the *other* side of the Rio Grande!"

"Why is she coming *here*?" asked Deputy Uniqua.

"I heard that she's coming to challenge the sheriff to a draw," said Tyrone. "She intends to find out once and for all who really is the fastest drawer in the West."

WANTED

TASHA THE KID

SHERIFF

Sheriff Pablo stood up, knocking over his chair. "What'll I do? What'll I do?" he squeaked. "What if she really *is* faster than me?"

"Sheriff Pablo."

"Then I won't be the fastest any longer, and . . ."

"Sheriff Pablo!"

"I'll have to give up all my trophies, and . . ."

"Sheriff Pablo!!" yelled his deputy. "The thing to do is practice."

"You're right," agreed the sheriff. "I'll go and practice."

Sheriff Pablo
glanced at the big
clock over the station house.
"It's nearly ten now!" he
gulped. "That means I only have two hours
to practice!" He raced away.

The townspeople gathered in the town square. "I hope the practicing is going OK," murmured Shopkeeper Tyrone.

The big clock over the station house ticked away.
At last, Austin the Barber looked up. "It's nearly noon!"

Dong! Dong! The clock began to strike!
Right on time, the train chugged into the station. Steam puffed and engines huffed.

"I surely hope the sheriff has been practicing!" whispered Barber Austin. "'Cause Tasha the Kid's about to get off of that-there train!"

Sheriff Pablo stood all alone in the middle of the deserted street. The clock finished striking.

The noon train pulled away. When the steam cleared, a lone figure stood facing the sheriff.

It was Tasha the Kid.

"Howdy Sheriff," she said. "I'm Tasha the Kid, and I'm the fastest drawer in the West."

"Howdy Kid," said Sheriff Pablo. "I'm Sheriff Pablo, and everyone around these parts knows that *I'm* the fastest drawer in the West."

"Looks like we need to find out who's *really* the fastest, Sheriff," said Tasha the Kid.

"Yep," replied Sheriff Pablo. "I reckon so."

The two stood back to back, as Deputy Uniqua
began counting.

They marched ten paces, then turned around to
face each other.

"Ready?" asked Deputy Uniqua, one finger on her stopwatch. Both of them nodded. The people of the town held their breath.

"Tell me what happens!" whispered Barber Austin, covering his eyes.

"DRAW!"

Tasha the Kid and Sheriff Pablo whipped out their drawing pads and began to draw. The only sound throughout the town was the furious scribbling of their pencils.

"Done!" yelled Sheriff Pablo.

"Done!" yelled Tasha the Kid, a second later.

For a second there was silence. Then the whole town erupted in cheers.

The sheriff was the quicker drawer!

"I guess fair is fair," Tasha the Kid said to Sheriff Pablo. "I didn't practice enough. You really *are* the fastest drawer in the West."

"Thanks," said the sheriff, holstering his pencil. "But your drawing is really good. You know what? Being a fast drawer isn't such a big deal. Being a *good* drawer is a mighty fine thing, too."

"You're *both* rootin'
tootin' drawers!" shouted
Barber Austin. "I'll hang both
drawings up in my barber shop!"

Sheriff Pablo's tummy rumbled.
"All that drawing's made me hungry," he admitted.
    "Why don't we go to my house and draw
ourselves up a snack?" suggested Tasha the Kid.
"I have lemonade and crackers!"

So everyone did just that.

Nick Jr. Play–to–Learn™ Fundamentals

Skills every child needs, in stories every child will love!

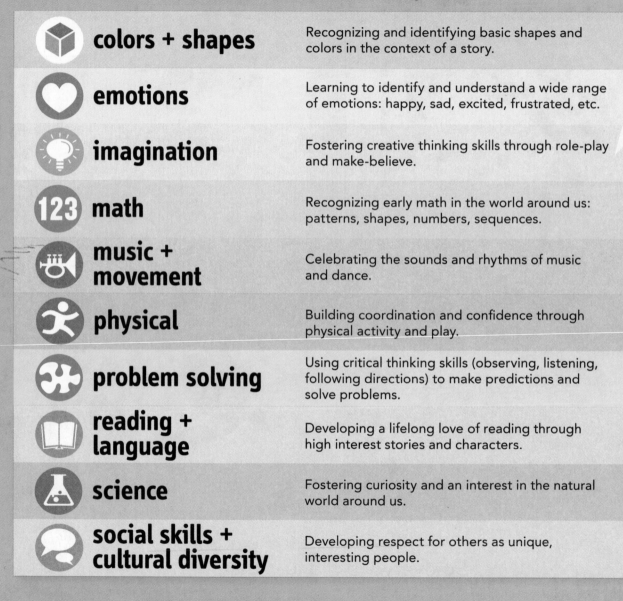

colors + shapes — Recognizing and identifying basic shapes and colors in the context of a story.

emotions — Learning to identify and understand a wide range of emotions: happy, sad, excited, frustrated, etc.

imagination — Fostering creative thinking skills through role-play and make-believe.

math — Recognizing early math in the world around us: patterns, shapes, numbers, sequences.

music + movement — Celebrating the sounds and rhythms of music and dance.

physical — Building coordination and confidence through physical activity and play.

problem solving — Using critical thinking skills (observing, listening, following directions) to make predictions and solve problems.

reading + language — Developing a lifelong love of reading through high interest stories and characters.

science — Fostering curiosity and an interest in the natural world around us.

social skills + cultural diversity — Developing respect for others as unique, interesting people.

Imagination

Conversation Spark

Questions and activities for play–to–learn parenting.

What would you do if you were Sheriff Pablo and found out that Tasha the Kid was coming to town? Practice for the big draw just like Sheriff Pablo did by drawing your favorite part of the story!

For more parent and kid-friendly activities, go to www.nickjr.com.